by Matthew K. Manning

illustrated by Joey Ellis

FAIRIES HATE PONIES

 raintree

a Capstone company — publishers for children

LEGEND SAYS . . .

The Rainbow-Barfing Unicorns
come from a faraway, magical
world called Pegasia. Not so
long ago, these stinky,
zombie-like, vomiting creatures
were banished to Earth for being,
well . . . stinky, zombie-like,
vomiting creatures. However,
Earth presents them with a new
danger: humans.

So, just who are the Rainbow-Barfing
Unicorns . . . ?

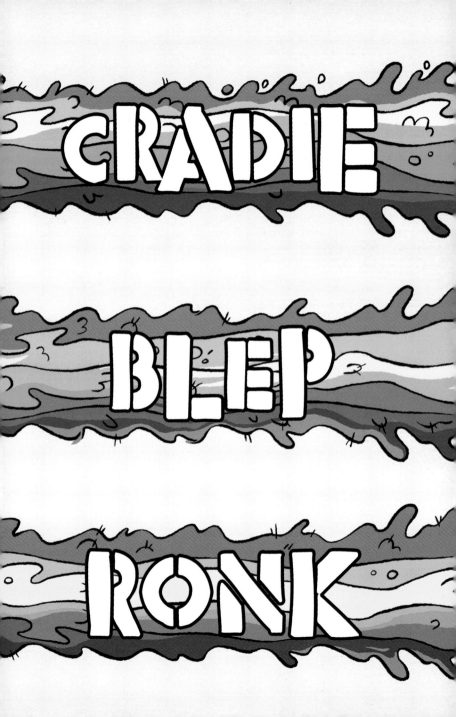

CHAPTER ONE

"Just give up!" Xander yelled. He stood facing the fence of the Henderson Landfill. His eyes narrowed. The target was in his sights. Xander had to time his actions perfectly, or all his efforts would be for nothing.

"Never!" screamed a figure from the shadows in front of him. "You won't take me alive!"

Xander smiled. *You should've stayed silent,* he thought. *I've got you now.*

Xander turned his weapon to spray mode and fired.

BWOOOOSH!

"Ah!" the creature screamed from the shadows. It stumbled forwards into the light of the setting sun.

The powerful blast was too much for the beast. The target lost its balance and fell to the ground.

Xander shook his head. He didn't want to smile, but he did anyway. "It's just a hose," Xander said. "You need a shower, Blep. Your smell gets even worse when you don't hose off."

The creature in front of Xander was the most difficult unicorn Xander had ever met. And surprisingly enough, though he was only twelve years old, Xander had met quite a few unicorns. The first few were Blep, Cradie and Ronk, who he'd discovered on the mountain behind his house. Since then, nothing in his life had been normal.

But Xander didn't mind. Magic was his speciality.

"I'm melting! MELTINNNNNG!" Blep said from the ground.

"No you're not, Johnny Dramatic," said Xander, rolling his eyes. "But you are getting your stage make-up cleaned off."

"I see a bright white light," Blep said. "I'm walking towards it. I see you, Mummy! I'm coming home!"

"PFFT! His mother is alive and well," said another unicorn, trotting out from behind a pile of broken television sets. It was Cradie. "She still lives in the mountains of Pegasia.

Really pretty countryside. Great view of the Custard River."

"I've missed you so much, Mummy! And I see Daddy too!" Blep continued.

Xander doubted Blep had ever seen a soap opera, but somehow the reddish unicorn was acting a lot like one.

"I'll be with you all again very soon," Blep moaned.

"His dad is fine, too," said Cradie. "He took us out for ice cream a week before we were banished to Earth."

Xander and Cradie both smiled.

Cradie had already showered off after the stage show. She hadn't made a big deal of it at all. There wasn't a hint of the make-up Xander had used to hide the cracks in her dry, flaking zombie skin. The hairspray he used to hold her shaggy mane was washed away as well.

Disguising the Rainbow-Barfing Unicorns as stage ponies in layers of make-up was the only way for them to fit in on Earth. When the unicorns were fully made up, no one knew they were really zombie unicorns from a world called Pegasia. People just thought that Xander put on the best magic show at the Montgomery Apple Orchard. (To be fair, he was the orchard's only magic show.)

Several months had passed since the Rainbow-Barfing Unicorns had been infected with a zombie virus and sent to Earth. Xander was happy to see Cradie finally joking about the experience. She seemed at home in her new life. And Xander was a big part of that comfort.

This planet couldn't compare to the sickly-sweet land of Pegasia. There, every meal was chocolate cake and sweets. But Earth certainly had its charm. Here at the Henderson Landfill, the Rainbow-Barfing Unicorns could safely hide and eat all the rubbish they could stomach. After all, Earth rubbish was the only food that a zombie unicorn could eat without barfing a rainbow.

In Xander's opinion, the Rainbow-Barfing Unicorns were actually helping his town's waste problem. Who needed a recycling centre when Cradie, Blep and their grey unicorn friend, Ronk, could make rubbish disappear?

BWOOOOSH!

Xander finished hosing off his difficult friend. He turned a switch near the nozzle and placed the hose on the ground. Then he picked up a towel from a pile of old rags and began drying Blep off.

"My whole life is flashing before my eyes," Blep cried. He locked eyes with Xander and added, "Tell Ronk he can have my collection of tuna tins."

"The problem is," said Xander, "you think you're funny."

"The problem is," said Blep as he stood up, "so do you, deep down."

Blep shook like a dog. Dirty water full of make-up and zombie rot sprayed across the fence. Xander did his best to leap out of the way, but his best wasn't good enough. Now he was the one who needed a shower.

"Well, thanks," Xander said to Blep.

Blep smiled while Cradie tried not to giggle.

"See you guys tomorrow," Xander said, faking anger. He waved as if annoyed and turned to walk towards the orchard's gate.

Xander's grin gave away his enjoyment, though. He always had a good time around the Rainbow-Barfing Unicorns, even when it wasn't in his best interest.

Once through the gate, Xander walked towards the car park at the other end of the orchard. His bike was parked outside, chained to the bike rack as usual. It was a nice summer night, and he was looking forward to the ride home. If nothing else, the warm wind would dry him off.

That's when Xander felt tiny feet land on his neck.

Xander's first thought was a single word: bee. The Montgomery Orchard was crawling with them. Bees were a part of the apple-growing process, and Xander was careful never to swat them. No bees meant no apple blossoms. No apple blossoms meant no orchard. No orchard meant no Rainbow-Barfing Unicorn show at the weekends. And that meant no spending money for Xander. This was Xander's own personal financial system, and he needed to protect it.

So Xander didn't swat at his neck. He froze in his bike tracks and waited for the bee to fly away.

But it didn't.

"Hey, buddy," said a small voice near Xander's ear. "What are you waiting for? I'm trying to catch a lift here."

Xander's eyes widened. He slowly turned to his left and then to his right. He didn't want to frighten the voice, but he wanted to find out who was talking to him.

"Hello?" he said.

He couldn't see a single person in the large open field. Xander was alone.

"C'mon, pal," said the voice again. "Get a move on."

The voice was coming from Xander's neck.

Slowly and cautiously, Xander reached his hand around over it – whatever it was – and gently lifted it off his neck.

So far so good. Nothing stung him.

Then Xander put his hand in front of his face and slowly uncurled his fingers.

Standing on his palm was a small, creepy creature. It had wings, four legs, two arms and what looked like the backside of a firefly. But it also had a face with a tiny, but talkative, mouth.

"What's the hold up?" said the insect-like creature. "I've got places to be."

Unfortunately for the little insect, Xander wouldn't be going anywhere anytime soon. In fact, he would spend the next three minutes staring at the creature in his hand with his mouth gaping open – all the while doing his best not to faint.

CHAPTER TWO

"This has been fun, but I'm a bit tired of staring at your face," said the insect-like creature after the three minutes had passed.

Xander looked down at him again as if for the first time. The shock had finally worn off. "You can talk," Xander said.

"I'm doing a better job of it than you at the moment," said the creature.

"What – what are you?" asked Xander.

"A rhinoceros," said the creature. "What does it look like?"

"Are you a . . . a fairy?"

"We like the term insect fairies, thank you very much," the fairy said, pacing on Xander's palm. He couldn't have been more than a few centimetres tall at most.

"Insect . . . ," Xander's voice trailed off. Suddenly, everything clicked.

Months ago, on the mountaintop behind Xander's house, Blep had mentioned insect fairies when he told Xander about how the Rainbow-Barfing Unicorns came to Earth. Xander hadn't questioned him, and he hadn't thought about them since.

"You're from Pegasia," Xander said at last.

"Yeah," said the insect fairy. "Wanna make something of it?"

"Oh, um, no," said Xander. "I just . . . I think you should come with me."

"Anything to get this bus moving," said

the fairy. Then the insect fairy folded his arms and took a seat on Xander's palm.

■ ■ ■

"Guys!" Xander shouted as he raced to the centre of the rubbish dump.

Over the last few weeks, the Rainbow-Barfing Unicorns had made themselves quite a set-up at the Henderson Landfill. Behind rows of broken fridges and mounds of rubbish bags, the unicorns had pushed several old sofas together. Next to those, they had arranged a beanbag chair, some broken coffee tables and even a greasy trampoline. It was their official living room of sorts, hidden away from curious visitors.

Cradie had named the spot Barf Central.

Xander tried not to call it that. But he knew that if the Rainbow-Barfing Unicorns weren't in the orchard's stable or performing, they were probably spending time there. And they were probably munching on something that smelled terrible.

"Where's the fire?" said Blep as Xander turned the corner into Barf Central.

"Hey," said Cradie. She was eating some rubbish covered in a thick layer of green and white mould. Xander wasn't sure he wanted to know what the rubbish had been originally.

"RONK!" said Ronk as he bounced on the trampoline.

"Guys, look at this!" Xander said, opening his hand towards them.

"Well that's some introduction," said the insect fairy. "I'm not a toy, you know. Whatever happened to manners in this dimension?" As the insect fairy said this, he scratched his backside with one hand. He sniffed his hand, made a disgusted face, and then scratched his backside again.

Blep walked over to Xander. "Oh," he said. "Hello."

"Hello," said the insect fairy. He had almost finished scratching his tail end at this point. Almost.

"Yeah, that's an insect fairy," Blep said to Xander.

"I know what it is," said Xander.

"It has a name, you know," said the fairy, annoyed.

"Oh, sorry," said Xander. "My name's Xander. What's yours?"

"Xander? What kind of silly name is that?" said the insect fairy.

"Excuse me?" Xander said, almost under his breath. He didn't want to offend his guest. (Although at the moment, he wasn't sure why he didn't want to offend him.)

"The name's Willibop. Nice to meet some of you," said the fairy.

"Xander is a better name than–" Xander muttered.

"Likewise," interrupted Blep. "Name's Blep and this is–"

"I know who you are," said Willibop. "Why do you think I'm here?"

"We don't know why you're here," said Cradie, walking over to Xander and the insect fairy. "Maybe you could fill us in."

"Sure, sister," said Willibop.

"Sister?" Now Cradie was the one muttering under her breath.

"Just sit back, and you're gonna hear the story of a lifetime," said Willibop. He was standing now, facing the gathered Rainbow-Barfing Unicorns. "This here's a tale for the ages. You can thank me later for finally bringing some excitement into your boring little lives."

"Um . . . OK?" said Xander.

"All right," said Willibop. "So I'm gonna start at the beginning . . ."

CHAPTER THREE

Basically, us fairies hate ponies. So to get away from them, we followed you slobs from Pegasia to Earth. The end.

CHAPTER FOUR

"I was thinking there'd be more to the story," said Xander. "Like, maybe a chapter's worth or something."

No one was listening to Xander at the moment. But he was used to that.

"That's it?" said Cradie. "Seriously?"

"Told you it was a great story," said Willibop.

The insect fairy squatted down on

Xander's hand and flapped his wings a few times. Then he shot up into the air! Willibop landed on one of the Rainbow-Barfing Unicorns' ripped sofas. He quickly made a tiny seat out of stuffing that was sticking out of a cushion.

"I've got a way with words," Willibop added. "Just naturally gifted, I suppose."

"That's one way to put it," said Cradie.

"So you guys hate unicorns," said Blep. "Let me guess, they drive you crazy with their sweet talk and fruit-flavoured smells."

"Give the pony a prize," said Willibop. He wasn't even looking at Blep at the moment.

"You're our guest here, so I let that name-calling go the first time," said Cradie. "But I don't want to hear it again."

"Name-calling?" asked Xander.

"We let you off because you don't know any better," said Blep. "But nobody calls unicorns 'ponies'. It's an insult."

"Oh," said Xander. His mind was currently thinking about damage control. Had he called the Rainbow-Barfing Unicorns ponies before? He couldn't remember now. Either way, his face started to get hot. Xander felt uncomfortably embarrassed.

"Didn't know I had to fly on eggshells around you pon–er, whatever," said Willibop. "Thought we were all in the same boat. You guys can't be fans of normal . . . unicorns either, right? I mean, they threw your tails outta Pegasia."

"We were infected by a zombie virus," said Cradie. "They had no choice but to banish us. We tried to eat them."

"Hey, if you go around smelling like strawberries somebody's bound to wanna take a bite out of you. That's what I always say," said Willibop.

Xander wondered who he always said that to. He doubted it came up much. But everybody had already seemed to move past that point.

"The fact is," Willibop continued, "you guys were all over the news in Pegasia. I heard about the portal to Earth, so I switched it on when no one was looking. I'm what you call a scout. I'm getting the lay of the land here, and I'm gonna report back later to my buddies. Let 'em know if the grass is greener, so to speak."

"This part of your story is longer than your actual story," Xander said.

Willibop didn't seem to hear him. Or if he did, he didn't feel like acknowledging him.

"So far, besides the three of you, there ain't no annoying ponies around here," said Willibop. "Nobody farting candyfloss. Nobody singing in a high-pitched voice. Nobody giggling at all hours of the night. This place seems pretty perfect to me."

"What did I tell you about that word?!" Cradie said. She hadn't been very welcoming to Willibop before. Now, there was no trace of kindness in her voice. Xander felt a bit nervous, and Cradie wasn't even mad at him.

"Yeah, yeah," said Willibop. "Didn't mean nothin' by it. Force of habit."

"Then change your habits," said Cradie.

"Wait, so you have a portal back to Pegasia?" asked Xander after a moment.

"Like I'm gonna come all the way here without checking a map first," Willibop said, laughing under his breath. "Are all humans this brainless?"

With that, Cradie walked over to the sofa. She lowered her head and pointed her horn at the fairy.

"Wow, somebody got up on the wrong side of the chocolate fountain this morning," said Willibop. "Listen, I gotta go anyway. Good talk."

Before anyone else could say anything, the insect fairy buzzed away. He was so small, Xander couldn't even see him after he had flown a few metres back towards the orchard.

"Was that really necessary?" asked Blep.

"Did you like that guy?" asked Cradie.

"What?" said Blep. "He spoke his mind."

Cradie didn't answer. She walked over towards a bag of rubbish and bit it open with her crooked teeth. Blep sat down on the sofa and Xander sat next to him.

"RONK!" Ronk said from his trampoline. He had been bouncing this entire time, blissfully unaware of the tension hanging in the air above the Henderson Landfill.

"Maybe I should go," said Xander.

"RONK!" Ronk said again. He wasn't answering Xander. He had finally fallen off the trampoline. That was his unique way of saying "ouch".

Xander took the exclamation as a message of agreement anyway. He stood up and waved to Cradie. "See you," he said.

Cradie just grunted as she found a half-eaten chocolate bar in her rubbish bag. Without thinking, she gobbled it up.

As Xander walked back to the orchard, he saw a beautiful rainbow light the sky. The sight was highlighted by the noise of Cradie yelling her own name. She did that every time she barfed a rainbow.

Somehow, it never got any less gross.

CHAPTER FIVE

Kelly sat underneath her favourite apple tree at the Montgomery Apple Orchard and Farm. It was the perfect shady spot, even on a hot morning like this one.

Xander could see her on that grassy hill. She sat still, with the blue mountains behind her and the sun behind them. He knew she wasn't a morning person. But this view had to make it worth getting up early to help out at her aunt's orchard.

Well, that and the bit of money her Aunt Melinda gave her every week.

Xander cleared his throat. He always did that when he wanted Kelly to notice him. When she turned around, Xander started to walk again. He wanted to look like he was just passing by. He always did that, too.

If Kelly was clever – and Xander knew she was one of the top pupils in his class – she had to be on to him by now. She had to know that he passed by this spot every Sunday because he knew she'd be here.

"Hey, Xander," Kelly said. Her smile told him that even if she was on to his scheme, it was OK. She apparently didn't mind his company.

"Oh, hey," said Xander. He stopped near a wheelbarrow full of apples. "I didn't see you there." (He totally did.)

"When does the show start?" Kelly asked. "I always forget." (Xander knew she couldn't forget. It was the same time every Sunday.)

"Midday," Xander replied. He kicked at a dirt patch with his shoe. It was the same dirt patch he kicked every time he stopped in that particular spot. His kicking was the reason there wasn't grass there in the first place.

"Oh," said Kelly. "So you're getting your ponies ready?" (Xander knew she knew that's what he was doing.)

"They don't like to be called ponies," Xander said. Then he froze. That was information that Kelly certainly did not know. In fact, the rest of the world didn't know he regularly chatted with unicorns.

Kelly laughed. "Did they tell you that?" she asked. She stood up from under the tree.

She had been taking too long a break and needed to get back to work.

"Um . . . no?" said Xander. His reply sounded like a question, so he corrected himself. "No," he said, more confident this time. "Of course not. It's not like they can talk or anything. That would be ridiculous."

Kelly wrinkled her brow. Xander was a strange boy. But she seemed to like that about him. "So then how do you know that they don't like to be called–" Kelly began, but then interrupted herself by swatting at the air.

Xander's eyes widened.

"I know I'm supposed to leave the bees alone," said Kelly. She was the embarrassed one now. "They just sort of . . . freak me out."

Xander walked closer to her. He wanted to make sure they were actually talking about a bee.

"Swatting makes it worse," he said in the meantime.

"I know," she said. "I can't help the reaction. I've been stung so many times you wouldn't believe it."

As Kelly talked, Xander noticed something in the tree branches above her head. Two small, insect-like creatures were buzzing around an apple. They seemed to be chasing each other, fighting over the ripe piece of fruit. They were most definitely not bees.

"You should get to work!" Xander found himself yelling.

"Oh," Kelly said, taken aback. She didn't expect nagging from Xander of all people. It's not like he ever had his nose to the grindstone, or even knew what a grindstone was, for that matter. "Um . . . yes, probably."

Now that he was a bit closer, Xander could tell that the two insect fairies above her head were definitely fighting. Luckily for everyone involved, they weren't talking. They were just making weird, alien buzzing sounds as they pushed and shoved at one another.

Then the smaller of the two leaped off the apple. He circled down close to Kelly's head. Then he charged at his fellow fairy, building up speed all the while. The larger of the two dodged the attack. He simply swatted the smaller one away.

"I just mean . . . ," said Xander. "Because of the bees!" He was talking way louder than the volume that this sort of conversation required. He couldn't help himself.

The smaller insect fairy was falling fast.

He was on a direct collision course with the top of Kelly's head.

"Bees!" Xander shouted.

Kelly took a step forward. Her brown eyes shot Xander a confused look.

The small insect fairy missed her head by a couple of centimetres. But Xander couldn't tell where he went. He glanced back up at the bigger of the two. That particular fairy had shoved his face into the apple. He was clearly the winner of the fight. He seemed pretty satisfied with himself as he munched on the apple. Xander thought that this one was even bigger than Willibop.

Kelly noticed Xander looking above her, and she moved to look up too. But before she could see what he was glaring at, Kelly felt Xander tugging at her arm.

"Lots of bees!" was all he said. His face was full of panic. So Kelly let him pull her away from the tree.

As they hurriedly walked, Xander looked her up and down.

"What?" she asked. "Xander, you're being really weird now."

"I thought I saw a–" He stopped talking when he noticed the smaller insect fairy trying to fight his way out of a lock of Kelly's brown hair. The little guy seemed stuck and frustrated.

"Is there a bee in my hair?!?" Kelly was the one that sounded panicked now.

"Um, yes . . . ?" Xander said in a long, drawn-out tone that got higher the longer he said it.

"Ah!" Kelly said. She jumped up and

down and shook
her head.

After being
slapped in the face
by Kelly's hair,
Xander regained
his senses. His
hand shot out. In
one quick motion,
he grabbed the
insect fairy and

then shot his hand into his pocket.

"Hey!" yelled the insect fairy in a
deep voice.

"What?" asked Kelly. She had calmed
down a bit. "Did you say something?"

"I said, 'Hey, I got the bee out'," said
Xander. It might have been the most

awkwardly spoken sentence in the history of all time.

"You did?" asked Kelly.

"Yep," Xander said. "Knocked it free. I just saw it fly off."

Kelly let out a sigh of relief. "Thank you," she said in the same exhale. "I'm such a little scaredy-cat."

Xander made a confused expression. Kelly was anything but a scaredy-cat. He'd once seen her catch a pair of snakes with her bare hands when they got too close to a guest at the orchard.

Then a voice brought him back to reality. "It's dark in here!" shouted the insect fairy from Xander's pocket.

"What?" said Kelly. She looked at Xander.

Kelly was pretty sure she hadn't seen Xander's lips move.

"I . . . I'm . . . hungry," said Xander. "My stomach's growling."

"I thought you said something," said Kelly.

"Because . . . ," Xander held the word, giving himself time to think. "Because you're hungry, too," he finally said.

"That doesn't make any–"

"OK, bye!" Xander blurted out.

Before Kelly could respond, she was alone there on the grass. She turned to watch Xander speed-walk towards the stable. On the way, he looked over at what seemed to be another bee. His hand shot out, and he grabbed it. Then he instantly opened his hand and shook it in pain.

"Xander?" she called after him.

"That one was definitely a bee!" he called back to her. Then he rushed away, holding his injured hand as he went.

CHAPTER SIX

Xander wanted ice or something soothing. His right hand was throbbing from the bee sting. Of course there was nothing like that in the stable. Nothing but a few old mattresses, some straw and some loose chocolate bar wrappers that had no doubt been the result of Ronk's sweet tooth.

Xander loved chocolate, but Ronk made him look like an amateur.

Xander couldn't think about chocolate or even his bee sting right now. He reached into his pocket with his other hand and retrieved the insect fairy.

Now free from the prison of Xander's pocket, the fairy sat down on Xander's bent thumb.

"I'd run that thing under cold water or something," said the fairy. He nodded at Xander's other hand. "You should see what a bee sting does to somebody my size."

"Who are you?" Xander asked.

"Grindini," said the insect fairy. "And you're the kid with the silly name."

"My name is Xander," said Xander.

"Exactly," said Grindini. "You've got some mean parents, kid, to stick you with a name like that."

Xander was going to respond but thought better of it. Instead, he changed the subject. "How are you here?"

"Came through the portal," said the insect fairy.

"Well, yeah, I guessed that. But, I mean, why?" asked Xander.

"Cause Willibop told us this place is awesome and that there are only three, slightly annoying ponies–"

"Unicorns," Xander corrected him.

"–slightly annoying unicorns living here instead of hundreds," said Grindini. "So me and my cousin Bobosnodo thought we'd check this place out."

"Oh," said Xander. He wasn't sure what to say. This wasn't great.

"And Willibop was right," said Grindini.

"Apples as far as the eye can see. Clean air. No candyfloss clouds blocking out the sun. No constant sounds of unicorns farting blueberries. Just peace and quiet."

"Well, yeah, but–" Xander began.

"I mean, me and Bobosnodo were thinking of just visiting," Grindini interrupted, "but now I'm starting to think again." The insect fairy stood up and stretched. His four tiny feet tickled the side of Xander's hand – so much so that Xander almost dropped him.

"You don't mean you'll live here?" Xander asked. He didn't mean for it to sound insulting. But it certainly did sound that way.

"What's it to you?" Grindini said.

"I mean . . . it's just . . . ," Xander

stammered. "People can't know you exist, you know? Magic is a secret here."

"Listen, kid," said Grindini. He flapped his wings at a rapid pace and began to hover in the air. He raised himself until he was right in front of Xander's eyes. "I'll tell it to you like my ma told it to me," he said. "Secrets don't make friends."

Then Grindini quickly turned and flew out of the stable door.

Xander looked around at the empty, shady room. At least his hand had stopped hurting so much.

CHAPTER SEVEN

Cradie was looking at Xander through serious eyes. The look terrified him, if he was being honest. Cradie's eyes were usually so full of life. Despite the fact that she was officially undead and everything, Cradie was a pretty lively unicorn. So when her eyes matched her exterior, Xander knew it was time to worry.

"This is not good," Cradie said.

Xander nodded.

"This is really not good," Cradie repeated.

The purplish unicorn paced in front of
the Barf Central sofas. Blep was lying on
one of those very sofas at the moment, as
was Ronk.

Ronk seemed to be asleep, but his eyes
were wide open. It was always hard to tell
what Ronk was doing. The day was nearly

over now, and after today's show, it made sense that Ronk would be tired. But with him, things could go either way. Sometimes he was most awake in the middle of the night. Just last week he'd woken up at two in the morning and tried to get Cradie to play a game of hoofball with him. In response, she swiped his ball and used it as a pillow.

Blep's eyes were closed. But unlike Ronk, Xander knew that he was definitely awake. Xander could tell, because Blep was currently grunting.

"I don't see the big deal," Blep said. "I mean, we moved here, why can't they? Free country and all."

"People are going to see them!" Xander exclaimed. "They'll know they're magical creatures!"

"Yeah," said Blep. His eyes were still closed. "So?"

"How long before they put two and two together?" Cradie said, turning those serious eyes to Blep. "How long before everyone finds out we're magic, too?"

"Still not seeing the big deal," said Blep. He opened his eyes and stood up. He yawned and then chomped his teeth together twice.

"I know you don't have people in your dimension," Xander explained, "but humans, well, we are easily scared."

Blep hopped off the sofa and stretched.

"If people see real unicorns . . . zombie unicorns . . . they'd lock you guys up in a heartbeat," Xander continued. "They'd run tests to see what makes you tick. I don't know how far they'd go. But it's safe to say you'd be in a cage for the rest of your . . . life?" Xander paused, and then said, "Are you guys officially alive? I can never keep it straight in my mind about zombies . . ."

"Either way, I'm not happy to be a science experiment," said Cradie. "If the insect fairies can't keep their mouths shut around humans . . ."

"You guys keep saying these insect fairies are so rude," said Blep. "And sure, that Willibop guy could use a lesson in manners. But you're judging every single fairy by the way a couple of 'em act."

Cradie was about to respond, but she stopped herself. For once, Blep was actually making a kind of sense. Maybe she was being too judgemental.

"Speaking of bad apples," Blep said. "Time for a snack."

He walked over to his secret stash, a rusty metal tray behind the sofa. The tray always contained a pile of Blep's current favourite treat: rotten apples. He spent an hour or two after the Orchard closed every night meandering through the rows of trees to find apples that were on the ground. But that was only one of his requirements. Each apple had to be just rotten enough so that it wouldn't hurt his stomach and make him barf a rainbow the way fresh food did.

The orchard had just closed a few minutes ago. In less than an hour, Blep would begin his nightly rounds. It must have been calming for him. There were no humans to scream at the zombie unicorn or to want to pet an overly made-up "show pony". It was just Blep, a setting sun and the hidden treasure of rotten fruit.

"Hey!" Blep shouted from around the corner. "Which one of you lot ate my apples?"

Xander and the Rainbow-Barfing Unicorns knew that Blep's apple stash was his prized possession. No one was silly enough to steal it. Xander certainly didn't want worm-ridden fruit, often slightly smooshed with a shoe print. Cradie and Ronk were just as happy eating rubbish straight out of the bag. So Blep knew the answer to his question before he yelled it.

"Not me," said Cradie.

"**RONK,**" said Ronk. He was awake now. Or Xander thought he was. Ronk's eyes were open, but he still wasn't moving. He could be talking in his sleep for all Xander knew. In fact, that seemed highly likely at the moment.

"Gross," said Xander, to answer Blep's question.

Blep knew his friends were telling the truth. But that just raised more questions.

Suddenly his ears twitched. "Do you hear that?" Blep said in almost a whisper.

"RONK!" Ronk said again. Xander was sure Ronk was sleeping now.

Blep walked out of Barf Central, tracking some unheard sound. Cradie followed, and Xander took up the rear. Ronk began snoring, so Xander assumed he wouldn't be coming with them. But a second later, Ronk was hot on his heels, his eyes closed now.

Even weirder, Ronk was still snoring.

Blep kicked open the gate that stood between the landfill and the orchard. Then he froze in his tracks.

"Oh," he said. Such a quiet response seemed very unlike the usually outspoken Blep. So Xander walked closer, and strained his head around the gate to see what he and Cradie were staring at.

In front of him stood the rolling hills of the Montgomery Apple Orchard. But the trees seemed to be moving. Xander squinted. Upon closer inspection, the trees weren't moving at all. They were covered in insects.

No, not insects. Insect FAIRIES.

The entire orchard was overrun with them! There were thousands of tiny creatures, shoving and pushing each other.

They were after apples, and each insect fairy was prepared to throw a couple of punches to make sure his belly was filled. Even the rotten apples on the ground were being fought over by the pushy winged creatures.

"Looks like we know where your apples went," said Cradie.

"Huh," said Blep. "I'm starting to see your point."

CHAPTER EIGHT

The good news: the Montgomery Apple
Orchard and Farm was closed on Mondays.
Seeing as she worked at the weekends, Kelly's
Aunt Melinda needed at least one day off
a week. Monday was her day to sleep in at
her home in the town of Henderson. She
never ventured to the farm on that day, no
matter what. So that meant Xander and the
Rainbow-Barfing Unicorns had a full day

to get the insect fairies out of the orchard without worrying about anyone discovering the magical creatures.

The bad news: they only had one day to get thousands of insect fairies out of the orchard. That didn't seem ideal to Xander. In fact, it didn't really seem humanly possible.

"Willibop!" Cradie yelled as she galloped through the rows of trees on Monday morning. "Willibop!"

She had been doing this for a good five minutes.

Xander was following her. He was trying to stay as close behind her as possible but had been struggling to do that since about the one-minute mark.

"Willibop!" Cradie yelled. At the end of the row, Cradie stopped herself before she accidentally ran into Ronk and Blep.

"Found him," Blep said. Then he nodded towards Ronk.

On the tip of Ronk's nose stood Willibop. The tiny insect fairy looked even more annoyed than usual.

"You wanted to see me?" Willibop said. He was standing on his back legs. He had his arms crossed. His second set of legs were crossed as well.

As soon as Xander caught up with the group, he began wondering whether or not he had been mistaken. Maybe that wasn't Willibop's second set of legs. Maybe it was a second set of arms. He got so distracted thinking about the subject that he missed the beginning of the conversation.

As Xander reached them, Cradie was saying, "At this rate, you're going to devour every apple in the place by Tuesday!"

"Nah," said Willibop. "I say the place will last at least until the weekend. Then we can move on. This planet has to be packed with these orchard things, right?"

Xander looked over to the closest apple tree. There were at least a hundred insect fairies buzzing around it. At least twenty of them seemed to be involved in some sort of wrestling match over a particularly red apple.

"Are all insect fairies this–" he began.

"This what?" said Willibop. "I'd choose your words carefully, Mr Funny Name."

"No, Xander. They're not all like this," said Cradie. Then she turned to Willibop. "I'm actually amazed at how rude all your friends are."

"Listen, if you don't like the way me and my cousins act, that's your problem, not ours, Purple," said Willibop. "The fact is, most insect fairies, they love all that sickly-sweet nonsense. And yes, we miss the food in Pegasia. I mean, everything's edible there. But me and mine, well, we're happier where the only thing sweet is what you eat."

"Wait, these are all your relatives?" asked Xander. He looked around at the thousands of insect fairies buzzing around him.

"That's right," said Willibop. "What? Ain't no crime having a big family."

"Listen," said Blep, finally speaking up. "I get it, Willibop. I'd be lying if I said I had a hard time keeping my lunch down in Pegasia. And that's not just 'cause us zombies barf rainbows if we eat anything other than rubbish." Blep locked eyes with Willibop. "But there just ain't enough food here to go around."

"Nah," said Willibop. "But there's enough to last a week, like I said."

"And by then," said Cradie, "a few hundred of you will have spoken in front of the humans. And people will know that magic is real. Then they'll round us unicorns up and–"

"OK, OK," said Xander. He stepped

between Cradie and Willibop. "Let's compromise."

"I'm a reasonable fairy," said Willibop. "What have you got in mind, kid?"

"You guys are welcome to stay here," said Xander.

"No they're not!" yelled Cradie.

"You're welcome to stay here under one condition," Xander continued.

"Not sure you're in a position to make the rules," said Willibop, "but I'm gonna let you finish."

"None of you talk," said Xander. "Not a peep. And when visitors get here tomorrow, you don't let them get a good look at you. You keep buzzing, you keep flying around. But you don't stop near them so they can see you up close."

"I'm not into hiding who I am, kiddo," said Willibop.

"You're eating the apple supply of an entire orchard that doesn't belong to you," said Xander.

"Yeah, but–" Willibop began.

"But nothing," Xander said. He was surprised by his own boldness. "Pegasia belongs to you guys. You can eat whatever you want there. But here on Earth – this particular property at least – it belongs to my friend's aunt. So the least you can do before you put her out of business is to keep to yourselves and not bother her paying customers."

Cradie and Blep must have been surprised by Xander's confidence, too, because neither said anything.

Willibop exhaled loudly. Then he said, "Deal."

As the insect fairy buzzed away, Cradie turned to Xander. "OK, so that solves part of our problem. But we're still going to be out of a job and a home by the weekend if they devour the orchard."

"Right," said Xander. "So we'd better make those posters fast."

Without explaining himself, Xander began to run towards the front gate of the orchard. Running, much like standing up straight, was again not something Xander was known for. So the Rainbow-Barfing Unicorns trotted after him without question.

CHAPTER NINE

"This could get you sacked, right?" asked Cradie from the back of Xander's bike trailer.

Xander was puffing a bit too hard to answer at the moment. Hauling all three Rainbow-Barfing Unicorns was pretty hard for him. Luckily, the top of the hill was in sight, and soon he'd be coasting the rest of the way to Henderson.

After he reached the top of the hill, Xander finally answered. "We won't – huff – have a job anyway if we don't – huff – try something."

Cradie nodded her head. Xander explained the plan to her before he was out of breath, so there wasn't really anything else to say. This was either going to work, or it wasn't. But it seemed to be the only way to rid the orchard of Willibop's family of insect fairies.

Minutes later, Xander turned onto the Main Street of the small town. Cradie bit the blanket Xander kept in the back of the small bike trailer. With Blep's help, the two spread the blanket over their heads. It was pretty warm underneath the wool covering, but it was necessary. None of the Rainbow-Barfing

Unicorns were wearing stage make-up. They didn't want to frighten any Henderson locals by appearing in town in all their rotting zombie glory.

"**RONK,**" Ronk complained from under the blanket.

"Shh," Cradie said. But she understood. It was stuffy under there, but the smell was even worse than the heat.

Xander stopped his bike by a bike rack. He jumped off and chained it up. He was still moving at a speed usually alien to him. It was almost midday, and they needed to get this done quickly if there was any chance for the plan to work.

Xander ran into the small office supply shop on the corner and straight back to its even smaller photocopying centre.

He slapped a piece of paper on the counter and said to the teenager behind it, "Two hundred copies!"

The teenager picked up the piece of paper, shrugged, and then got to work.

■ ■ ■

Xander's bike was in the shade, but it didn't matter too much at that point. All three of the Rainbow-Barfing Unicorns had decided to nap. It turned out that the blanket was more cosy than stuffy thanks to the day's cool breeze.

Cradie, Blep and Ronk thought that while Xander ran around town, they may as well take the opportunity for some shut-eye. After all, their day had been a pretty full one.

They had rested, grazed on rubbish and then been passengers in a bike trailer. How could they be expected to do anything but sleep?

Meanwhile, Xander paced up and down Main Street. Every person he saw was handed a photocopied piece of paper. He even accidentally gave a flier to the same woman twice, first when she went

into a shop and later when she came out.
Xander didn't have much choice. He had
to get the word out. The very existence of
the Montgomery Apple Orchard and Farm
depended on it.

If the orchard closed its doors, that meant
Xander was out of a job. And if Xander was
out of job, that meant no more walking
casually by Kelly's special spot on Sunday
mornings. To Xander, not seeing Kelly at
the weekends was worse than not having
spending money. And he loved, loved,
loved spending money.

After dropping fifty fliers off at the pet
shop and then decorating the windscreens
of every car in a large car park, Xander
was down to his last few pieces of paper. He
rushed into the office supply shop again,

bought a roll of heavy clear tape and then rushed back out to the street. One by one, he taped a flier to every lamp post he could find.

By the end, Xander was sweating and out of breath. He could only hope the effort would be worth it.

Fortunately, he had a bit of money left. Which was perfect, because he wasn't just exhausted, he was also starving. To a twelve-year-old, that only meant one thing: chocolate bars. He had just enough money to buy three of them from the nearby petrol station.

"Whatcha got there?" came a voice from under his blanket when Xander returned to his bike.

"Really?" he said to Blep, who was

sticking his nose out.

"What?" said Blep. "I'm starving. You think all this waiting is easy on a unicorn?"

Xander sighed. He took a bite of his chocolate. Then he handed the rest to Blep.

Blep devoured it in one gulp.

Xander unwrapped his second bar. Ronk's nose slipped out of the blanket,

followed by Cradie's. Xander sighed again. Then he handed them each a chocolate bar.

As Xander pedalled back up the hill, chocolate-less and tired, three distinct rainbows trailed behind his bike.

Xander pretended not to notice.

CHAPTER TEN

Xander woke up early on Tuesday morning, surprising his mum and dad for the second day in a row. Getting up for his Rainbow-Barfing Unicorn shows on Saturday and Sunday was one thing. It was tough enough for Xander to do that, especially during these summer months. But the fact that Xander was voluntarily waking up early two summer weekdays in a row – that was just mind-blowing to his parents.

To them, Xander was a like a reverse bear. He slept all summer and was forced to stay awake all winter. It was certainly strange to see his hibernation interrupted like this.

"You're up again?" his mum asked him when he hurried downstairs.

"No time to talk!" Xander said. "Got stuff to do at the orchard!"

Before she could ask any other follow-up questions, Xander was already out of the door and on his bike.

This wasn't her son turning over a new leaf. This was her son investing in a leaf blower and turning over the whole garden!

"Have a good day!" she called after him. Xander managed a quick wave. He swerved his bike as a result, nearly crashing into the neighbour's garden fence.

Xander couldn't see her, but he was sure his mother was shaking her head as she watched him ride away.

■■■

"Would you care to explain this, young man?" Aunt Melinda said. Her hands were on her hips. It was a gesture Xander couldn't ever remember her making before.

In her hand, Melinda held a copy of one of Xander's fliers. But it was more in Xander's face than just in Melinda's hand at the moment. She wanted to make sure Xander could see it, which didn't make that much sense. He had made the flier in the first place. Of course he knew what it said.

"Um, no thank you?" Xander said.

Melinda lowered the piece of paper.

"Xander, this is not OK. The orchard has just opened and already we're packed to the gills with people who are expecting free stuff."

(Xander didn't know an orchard had gills.)

"Not only that," said Melinda, "but there's some sort of weird bug infestation going on."

"Really?" Xander asked. He tried to pretend as if he had no idea what she was talking about. Luckily for him, Melinda wasn't looking at his guilty face. She was pointing to a row of nearby Granny Smith trees.

"Look there," she said. "At the tops of the trees. Swarms of something. I can't tell what they are. But swarms are never a good thing for an orchard."

Xander pretended to be surprised. If he had been acting in a TV programme, a director surely would have yelled cut and called for a retake.

"And now we have all these new people here seeing these bugs," she said. "They'll think it's always like this!"

Xander didn't respond. He was currently working on another version of his surprised face. The director would have got rid of him at this point in the production.

"We need to sit down and talk about this later. I don't even want to know how much money we're losing," Melinda said. It didn't seem like she was really talking to Xander any more. It was more like she was talking to herself. Xander noticed this, because as she spoke, Melinda was walking away from him.

Xander stood in place there at the front gate to the orchard. He looked around at the car park. It was absolutely packed. He wondered what things were going to look like inside.

In front of him, Aunt Melinda had dropped the flier she was carrying. Xander walked over and picked it up. He looked at his scribbled illustration of a puppy. It wasn't that bad, he told himself. After all, he hadn't had a lot of time to work on the drawing.

Above the drawing, he read the words: "This Tuesday Only! The Montgomery Apple Orchard and Farm. All people accompanied by puppies, kittens or babies recieve all the apples you can pick – absolutely free!"

Xander cringed. He had got the spelling wrong for "receive".

CHAPTER ELEVEN

"Aren't you the cutest widdle person in the whole wide world?" Kelly said in a voice higher pitched than Xander had ever heard her use. "Wes you are! Wes you are!"

She was lying on the grass, her legs bent up behind her. In front of her on a red blanket, crawled a baby. The baby was doing his very best to make it to Kelly before he collapsed under the weight of his rather large head. He didn't quite make it. But the spill caused Kelly to giggle in that same high-pitched voice.

"Oopsie daisy!" she said.

The confused baby pushed himself back up. He locked his elbows for a second and then collapsed again.

"I think that's enough exercise for now," said a man who must have been the baby's father. He was sitting on the blanket behind the baby. He tucked his hands under the child's arms and moved the excited little boy to his lap.

"Oh, what a cutie!" Kelly said. She sat up, just in time to be tackled by a puppy. She giggled that high-pitched giggle again. Xander wasn't sure if this was a good thing or a bad thing. It certainly was a new thing.

After wrestling with this puppy she'd never seen before for a full minute, Kelly sat up and placed the dog back on its paws. It wagged its tail before hearing a familiar voice.

"Chester!" the voice called. The puppy's ears perked up. As quickly as the dog had appeared, it was gone. Finally, Xander had his opening.

Kelly was standing up and dusting herself off by the time Xander made his way over to her. When she finally noticed him, Kelly beamed a huge smile.

"This is your best idea ever!" she said. She had lowered the pitch of her voice just enough to sound close to her usual self.

Xander returned her smile and said, "Having fun?"

"Am I having fun?" Kelly said. "This place is crawling with babies, puppies and kittens! It's like every cute internet video has got together and hosted the world's most adorable event. How did you convince Aunt Melinda to do this?"

"I sort of just did it," said Xander.

"Oh wow," said Kelly. She was laughing now. "You are going to be in so much trouble."

Xander made a worried face, but he was still smiling.

It didn't matter. Kelly wasn't looking at him any more. She was now busy rushing over to a group of kids who each carried a tiny kitten. There seemed to be an entire litter of both.

Kelly was making some sort of

out-of-this-world squeal at this point, so Xander decided to give her space. He looked around. There were three puppies chewing at each other's ears under the nearest tree. To his left a baby was stealing his twin's sunglasses. To his right, a kitten smacked a baby in the face with its soft paw.

"You," said a stern voice behind Xander. "You've got some explaining to do, kid."

Xander turned around and found himself face to face with Willibop.

Xander gulped.

CHAPTER TWELVE

"What are you trying to do?" Willibop barked.

"Um, nothing?" Xander said.

Xander had managed to convince Willibop to wait until they were back at Barf Central before they continued their "conversation". And by "conversation", apparently that had meant "angry yelling".

It wasn't just the two of them in the dump

at the moment, though. Cradie, Ronk and Blep had already been sitting on the sofas when Xander got there. And the more Willibop yelled, the more insect fairies buzzed over to see what all the noise was about.

Luckily for Xander, none of the human visitors at the Montgomery Orchard seemed to care about the noise in the dump. They were too busy gushing over a cuteness overload and the opportunity for free apples.

"So me and my family here, we outright tell you that we can't stand cute stuff, right? I mean, you were there for that part of my story, weren't you?" Willibop asked in a harsher tone than Xander had expected. And it wasn't like Willibop had a soothing voice to begin with.

"Well, yeah–" said Xander.

"We told you we escaped Pegasia, a place that's virtually a wall-to-wall, all-you-can-eat buffet to come to this place to avoid all that stuff, right?"

"But–" Xander tried to interrupt.

"And we get here, and you tell us there's no ponies apart from the three creepy half-decomposing ones," said Willibop.

"Unicorns," Xander corrected.

"Everything's going great, I invite the extended family and then, boom, today the whole place is brimming with the exact same sort of squeaky-clean adorableness that we were trying to get away from in the first place."

Xander didn't reply this time. Nothing he said seemed to be registering with Willibop anyway.

"That was a low-down, dirty trick you pulled, Captain GoofyName," said Willibop.

"Xander is not a goofy name–" Xander began.

"Did you think I wouldn't find out?" Willibop said.

The insect fariy hovered closer to Xander's face. For someone only a few centimetres tall, Willibop was pretty intimidating when he wanted to be. Behind him, a few hundred of his closest relatives buzzed closer as well. Xander felt his palms start to sweat. He hadn't really thought this part of the plan through.

"Um," was all Xander could say.

"Why didn't you tell us that your dimension is even CUTER than Pegasia?"

Xander didn't answer. Was it possible that his plan was actually working?

"Well you've gotta get up pretty early in the morning to pull one over on old Willibop," said the angry insect fairy. "I don't know why you were trying to convince us to stay here and eat your apples – which aren't nearly as sweet as they should be, by the way – but we ain't falling for it."

"Oh . . . OK?"

"You bet your ridiculous name it's OK," said Willibop. With that, he turned to face his fellow fairies. "All right, cousins, we're outta this nightmare. Let's head back to Pegasia. At least there the cuteness is limited to one species."

"Good riddance," Blep said as Willibop flew off. Xander noticed he had waited until the insect fairy was well out of earshot to make his comment.

Cradie jumped off the sofa and trotted over to Xander. "I can't believe that worked," she said.

"Imagine if Willibop had it right," said Blep, "and it was this cute here every day. I'd be right behind those guys. I mean, have you heard the voices humans use when they talk to babies?" Blep shivered.

Xander looked at his friends. "I suppose all that's left to do is have that sit-down talk with Melinda," he said. "No point in putting it off."

As Xander walked away, Blep shivered again.

CHAPTER THIRTEEN

Xander sat at the desk opposite Aunt
Melinda in the small room that passed for
her office. It was located in the only proper
building at the orchard. Xander had been
in the building once in the whole time he'd
worked at the orchard – and that was just to
fill in some paperwork when he started the
job. He doubted Melinda had used the office
much more herself.

"So," said Melinda. She was sitting back in her chair. Something about her serious expression mixed with her straight, grey hair and the room's harsh artificial lighting made her appear much scarier than Xander thought possible. "First, I want to say that I was a little flustered when we spoke earlier," she said. "I had just found your flier, and I was too busy dealing with the crowds to think straight."

"I can explain–" Xander began.

"Let me finish."

"OK," he said.

"But, as things started to calm down, and I heard all the laughter and saw all the pictures being taken, and after all those people apparently scared away whatever type of bug was nesting in the trees," said Melinda, "well it started to make sense."

"It did?"

"You were taking the lead, Xander," said Melinda. She was almost smiling now. "You realized that a big promotion, one with kids and pets and whatever else that silly flier said . . . you realized that it would show people what a wonderful place we have here. And yes, we might have lost a little money on those apples you promised, but the free advertising alone . . . Did you know two local news crews turned up today? You can't buy that type of press. And I have your weird little posters to thank for it."

"Um . . . you're welcome?" said Xander.

"No, you're welcome," said Melinda, "because I'm not sacking you for that stunt. And you're not in trouble, either."

"Oh," said Xander. Aunt Melinda had finished talking now. It was his turn, but he didn't have anything to say.

After a moment passed, Melinda said, "Well go on. Get out of here. Go and feed your ponies or something."

"They hate it when you call them ponies," Xander said. He made it through the entire sentence before he realized he hadn't meant to say it at all.

"Just get out of here before I change my mind," said Melinda.

So Xander did just that.

■ ■ ■

On his way back to the dump, Xander saw Kelly. She had just finished stroking a cat that looked as if it didn't like being stroked.

"Hey!" she called when she saw him.

"Hey," he said.

"So, do you want to hear something weird?" Kelly asked.

"Always," said Xander. It might have been the first honest thing he'd said in the last hour.

"Did you see those weird bees circling the apple trees today?"

Xander nervously stuck his hands into his pockets. "Um . . . yes?"

"So, they all just flew off, like an hour or so ago," Kelly said.

"OK."

"Like all of them, together," she said.

"Yeah?"

"But that's not the weirdest part," said Kelly.

Xander was cringing. He didn't know he was cringing, but that's exactly what he was doing.

"As they flew away, one dipped down low, really close to me."

Xander didn't say anything. His palms were sweating again.

"And I swear – this is going to sound really crazy, but I swear – it had a mouth," said Kelly. "Like, a person's mouth. Not like a bee's mouth or whatever."

"Oh," said Xander. What was it that other fairy, Grindini, had said? "Secrets don't make friends." Maybe it was time for Xander to come clean with Kelly. Time to tell her all about the Rainbow-Barfing Unicorns and the insect fairies and Pegasia and everything.

"There's something you should know," Xander began. "I haven't been telling you the whole–"

"Ah!" Kelly screamed in Xander's face. He stepped backwards, wondering what he'd done to upset her. She couldn't have guessed about the zombies, could she? That was the kind of news a person actually had to hear out loud.

Then he saw what she was screaming at. To his right, a kitten was riding on the back of a rather large puppy. Both animals seemed confused about how they'd got into this predicament. Before Xander could say anything more, Kelly was almost tackling the animals. She stroked them with speed he didn't think was humanly possible.

"I suppose . . . we'll talk about it later," Xander said, pretty much to himself. He turned to walk back to the dump.

On his way, he spotted a rotten apple lying on the ground. He picked it up and put it in his back pocket. Blep would appreciate the afternoon snack.

As he walked, Xander didn't hear the muffled voice coming from his pocket. "Hey!" said an insect fairy. "What idiot has switched off the lights?"

CHARACTER SPOTLIGHT:
WILLIBOP!

Species: Insect fairy

Height: 5 centimetres

Length: 10 centimetres

Wing span: 15 centimetres

Colour: Yellow, orange and magenta

Like Rainbow-Barfing Unicorns, insect fairies come from the magical world of Pegasia. Unlike Rainbow-Barfing Unicorns, insect fairies HATE Rainbow-Barfing Unicorns. They can't stand them, in fact. That's pretty much it. The end.

GLOSSARY

dimension place in space and time

infestation spread or swarm of a harmful insect or pest

landfill system of waste disposal in which the rubbish is buried between layers of earth

orchard place where fruit or nut trees are grown

portal door or passage to another place

virus large group of very tiny organisms that can cause disease

BARF WORDS

blow chunks barf

heave barf

hork barf

hurl barf

puke barf

ralph barf

regurgitate barf

retch barf

spew barf

throw up barf

upchuck barf

vomit barf

yak barf

JOKES!!

How does a unicorn
tie its shoe?

With a rainbow!

What do you call a
rainbow over a farm?

A grainbow.

What street do
Rainbow-Barfing
Unicorns live on?

Mane Street.

Why are Rainbow-Barfing
Unicorns so rude?

They don't have any
stable manners.

How long should a
unicorn's legs be?

Long enough to
reach the ground!

READ THEM ALL!

AUTHOR

The author of more than seventy-five books, Matthew K. Manning has written several comic books as well, including the hit *Batman/ Teenage Mutant Ninja Turtles Adventures* miniseries. Currently the writer of the new IDW comic book series *Rise of the Teenage Mutant Ninja Turtles*, Manning has also written comics starring Batman, Wonder Woman, Spider-Man, the Justice League, the Looney Tunes and Scooby-Doo. He currently lives in North Carolina, USA, with his wife, Dorothy, and their two daughters, Lillian and Gwendolyn.

ILLUSTRATOR

Joey Ellis lives and works in North Carolina, USA, with his wife, Erin, and two sons. Joey writes and draws for books, magazines, comics, games, big companies, small companies and everything else in between.